The C.A.T.C.H. Files

#2 – The Area 51 Escape

Eugene Fuller

Copyright © 2026 FC Publishers
All rights reserved.
The Amazon Endure typeface was designed by 2K/DENMARK in 2025.
Template id: ST-414D415A-25-A01
Printed in The United States
ISBN: 979-8-9943996-4-4

DEDICATION

To our children who inspire us to look towards the stars.

TABLE OF CONTENTS

Prologue – The Night the Sky Broke

Nevada Desert, 1947

The ship was never supposed to touch the ground. Zara knew that the moment the stars went wrong.

"Something's pulling us," Kayo said, fingers flying across the glowing controls. His voice shook, but his hands stayed steady—trained, precise. "The navigation field is collapsing."

"That shouldn't be possible," Zara replied, gripping the edge of the console as the deck tilted beneath her feet. "We're outside any gravity well."

The stars stretched. Not blurred—*stretched*, like lines of light being dragged toward an invisible point.

The ship screamed. Not in sound, but in feeling. The walls vibrated with panic, light pulsing too fast, colors flashing warnings Zara had never seen before.

Kayo looked up at her, antennae flicking wildly. "Zara—"

"I know," she said. "I feel it too."

The comet tore past their viewport like a blade of fire. White-hot. Silent. Beautiful. And wrong! This was not supposed to be here. As it passed, space *folded*. The ship lurched violently. Alarms sang in cascading tones. Gravity flipped, then slammed back into place. Zara was thrown against the wall, breath ripped from her lungs.

“Kayo!” she shouted.

“I’m here!” he yelled back, scrambling upright. “We’re losing altitude—at least this planet has atmosphere!”

The viewport filled with brown and gold—desert rushing up far too fast. Zara slammed her palm against the emergency interface.

“Brace!” She yelled.

The world became noise. Metal shrieked. Light shattered. The ship struck the ground with a force that rattled Zara’s bones, skidding across sand and stone before finally slamming to a stop in a cloud of dust and fire. Then—

Silence.

Zara lay still, ears ringing, chest heaving. The lights dimmed to a soft, pulsing glow.

“Kayo,” she whispered. “Answer me!”

Silence.

Then a shaky laugh. “I think...I think my legs are backwards.”

Relief flooded her, “They are not.”

“They feel backwards,” he replied.

Zara pushed herself upright and crossed the cabin in three unsteady steps. She knelt beside him, checking his limbs, his antennae, his eyes.

“You’re intact,” she said.

"So are you," Kayo replied, forcing a smile. "That's good." The ship hummed weakly around them, wounded but alive. Zara turned toward the viewport. Lights flashed in the distance. Bright. Artificial. Moving fast.

Her stomach dropped. "We're not alone."

Kayo followed her gaze. "Who are they?"

Before she could answer, the night exploded with sound. Engines roared. Tires crunched over sand and rocks. Harsh white beams cut through the dust, pinning the ship in blinding light. Voices shouted—sharp, loud, afraid.

"Hands where we can see them!" One voice called.

"Circle the craft!" Came another voice. "Don't let anything come out!"

Zara flinched. "They're scared."

Kayo swallowed. "So am I."

The ship shuddered as something heavy struck its side. Metal clanged. Zara placed her hand over Kayo's. "We don't fight, we explain," she said.

"Yes."

The hull split open with a violent hiss. Cold desert air rushed in. Human figures poured into the opening—faces hidden behind helmets, weapons raised, eyes wide. Their fear burned hot and erratic, like sparks jumping between them. Zara lifted her hands slowly.

"We mean no harm," she said, speaking carefully, translating each word as she spoke.

The humans froze. One of them shouted, "Did you hear that?"

Another raised his weapon higher. "It's talking!"

Before Zara could say more, something struck her from behind. Her legs buckled. The world tilted. Kayo screamed her name. Darkness rushed in.

When Zara woke again, the air was cold. She lay on a narrow cot inside a bright, humming room. Metal walls. Harsh lights. No windows—except one. Thick glass. Beyond it stood humans in white coats, murmuring urgently. Kayo lay on a second cot across from her, awake, eyes fixed on the ceiling.

"You're back," he whispered.

"They didn't listen?" Zara said softly.

"No," he replied. "They definitely didn't listen, they tied us up. How rude."

Footsteps echoed outside. A door slid open with a hiss. A man stepped in carrying a tray. He was older than the others, shoulders rounded, eyes tired. His clothes were white like the rest—but stained, worn, real. He didn't meet their eyes at first. He set the tray down between them.

"I'm supposed to feed you," he said quietly.

Zara watched him. "Thank you."

He was startled, almost dropping the tray. "You talk?"

"Yes," she said gently. "So do you."

He swallowed hard and glanced toward the observation window. "Don't...don't talk too much."
Kayo tilted his head. "Why not?"

The man's mouth tightened. "Makes it harder."

Zara followed his gaze. Through a small, high window beyond the glass, the night sky was visible. And there...the comet burned across it. Slow. Majestic. Unstoppable.

Kayo sat up, antennae lifting. "It followed us."

Zara reached for his hand, squeezing it tight. "Then the window still exists."

The man noticed their focus and turned, frowning. "What are you looking at?"

"The sky," Zara said.

Kayo smiled faintly. "It means this will not last forever."

The man studied their faces—really looked at them for the first time. Not monsters. Not experiments. Just kids.

He exhaled slowly. "I hope you're right."

Zara leaned closer to Kayo and whispered, "It will be okay."

Kayo nodded. "Someone will come."

Outside, the comet burned on. And the desert remained still.

Chapter One – Quiet Things That Matter
Lincoln County, Nevada – Present Day

The kitchen smelled like onions, garlic, and something warm enough to make the whole house feel safer. When Gristle heard that the Bell family was in Navada. He had invited them over for dinner. He was also not surprised when they had Blaze with them. They had some planned event that Gristle knew in some way was important not only to them, but maybe to himself.

Gristle stood at the stove, sleeves rolled up, shoulders hunched the way they always were when he cooked—like he was guarding the food from the world. A heavy pot bubbled gently, steam fogging the window above the sink. He stirred slowly, deliberately, the wooden spoon scraping the bottom in a steady rhythm.

“Smells illegal,” Blaze said from the table. Blaze became a friend of the Bell family when he met them while camping at Whispering Pines in Washington state. He had helped with a case that the Bell family worked on to protect a Bigfoot family that was in danger of being caught and exploited.

Shortly after the Operation Bigfoot case was closed, and with the encouragement of the Bell family, Blaze submitted his application to become a junior agent of C.A.T.C.H. The Creatures Agency for Tracking, Conservation and Help.

The Bell family recommended him due to his technical expertise and keen observation skills that he showed during Operation Bigfoot. His performance as an applicant during whatever next case he worked on would determine whether he would be accepted as a junior agent.

Gristle didn't look up. "Good food should smell illegal."

Juniper Bell, the oldest child in the Bell family, sat on the counter, feet swinging. Milo Bell, her 9-year-old brother, was on the floor pretending to be a dog begging for food. Juniper was throwing marshmallows at him while he tried to catch them in his mouth. Milo had wanted a dog since he was 5 years old, but with the family's busy schedule as C.A.T.C.H. agents, it would be very difficult for them to take care of a pet.

Megan Bell, Milo and Junipers mother, leaned against the doorway, arms folded, watching the scene with a small smile. Emmett Bell, Megan's husband, sat at the table with Blaze, bits of paper and half-sketched diagrams spread out between them.

Blaze tapped a pencil against the table. "I'm just saying, if I reroute the power coupling through a redundant loop, the drone won't fry itself."

Emmett nodded appreciatively. "That's thinking ahead."

Juniper glanced at her dad. "You're encouraging him."

Emmett smiled. "I admire clever solutions."

Gristle snorted softly and reached for a ladle. It was dented and old. Its metal dulled by years of use.

Gristle, once an active C.A.T.C.H. agent, was the self-appointed cook, a change he made when a mission he was leading took a bad turn and he was blamed for the failure. To this day, he didn't know exactly what had happened and if he was truly to blame or not. The whole situation caused him to start doubting himself and he decided to step down from being an agent. Not wanting to turn his back on C.A.T.C.H. completely he offered his services as a cook on missions. The Bell family had grown to appreciate Gristle's grumpy sense of humor as well as his wise advice.

Milo noticed. "Hey, that's not your usual ladle."

Gristle paused. Just for a second. Then he stirred again. "Didn't always have usual."

The room quieted—not abruptly, but naturally, like everyone felt something shift and decided not to step on it. What did Gristle say?

Blaze looked up. "You okay?"

Gristle set the ladle down and reached for a smaller one from a hook nearby. "I'm fine."

Juniper tilted her head. "You're remembering."

Gristle glanced at her, surprised. Then he huffed a short laugh. "You're too observant for your own good, kid."

He leaned back against the counter, eyes on the pot, voice low. "My dad was a quiet man."

Milo looked up from the floor. "Quieter than you?"

Gristle smirked. "Much."

Megan moved closer, resting a hand on the counter. "You have never told us about him."

"He didn't talk much," Gristle said. "Didn't need to. You always knew when he was proud."

Blaze leaned forward. "How?"

Gristle lifted one shoulder. "He stood a little straighter. That was it."

He reached up and pulled open a high cabinet. Inside, neatly arranged, was a cooking set—old, polished, clearly cared for. Ladles of every size. Spatulas. Whisks. Even a pair of worn, medieval-looking warming knives wrapped in cloth.

Juniper's breath caught. "That's...."

"My dad gave it to me," Gristle said. "The night I told him I was going to join C.A.T.C.H."

Blaze blinked. "You told him?"

"Didn't know how not to," Gristle said. "Thought he'd ask questions. Thought he'd worry."

He shook his head. "He didn't say a word. Just stood up, opened that cabinet, and handed me this cooking set."

Milo wrinkled his nose. "Why did he give you cooking set?"

"He was a cook himself," Gristle answered. "He taught me to cook and said that he wanted me to have a good cooking set in case I needed a backup career."

Juniper noticed something missing. "You have one empty hook in your set. What is missing?"

Gristle nodded slowly. "One ladle isn't there."

Megan frowned. "What happened to it?"

"My dad said," Gristle continued, "that he gave that one to someone special. Someone that did something important."

The pot bubbled louder.

Gristle swallowed. “I didn’t ask who. Didn’t need to.”

Silence settled, warm and heavy.

“On nights like this,” Gristle said quietly, “I miss my dad.” Gristle turned back to his pot adding in more spices.

Milo scooted closer to Megan. “Mom?”

“Yes, Milo.”

“Can we get a pet?”

Megan didn’t even blink. “No.”

Milo’s shoulders slumped. “But—”

“Pets are a lot of responsibility,” she said gently. “They need time. Care. Attention and more time.”

Milo sighed dramatically and flopped onto the floor. “I am extremely responsible.”

Juniper snorted.

Blaze glanced at Emmett. “For the record, my inventions are also a lot of responsibility.”

Emmett chuckled. “Which is why we make sure you understand them before you build them.” Going back to Gristles topic Emmett said, “My dad was quiet too.”

Gristle glanced over. Emmett continued, voice thoughtful. “He didn’t say much about pride either. But he showed it by trusting me to make my own choices—even when he didn’t fully understand them. My dad was often mysterious. He made me promise that I would bring you kids here at this time to watch the meteor showers and see the comet. Why don't you come out and join us, Gristle?"

"That's a great idea" Megan Bell said slipping away from Milo to hand Gristle a bottle of spice he had been searching for.

Juniper smiled softly. "Guess some things tend to run in families."

Gristle turned back to the stove, picking up the ladle again. He stirred once, slow and steady.

"Some things," he said, "aren't loud."

The steam rose. The house felt full and comforting conversation of missions, old and new filled the air.

And somewhere between the clink of metal and the smell of dinner, a missing ladle waited to be found.

Chapter Two – The Desert That Remembers

The Nevada desert didn't feel empty at night. It felt like it was holding its breath. Juniper Bell lay on her back on a blanket that smelled like sun-warmed canvas and campfire smoke, her hands folded behind her head, her eyes fixed on the sky. Above her, the stars were sharper than anything she'd ever seen back home—like someone had taken the whole universe and scrubbed it clean. No streetlights. No porch lights. No phone screens glowing in windows. Just darkness, sand, and a sky so huge it made Juniper feel like she was tiny in the best possible way.

"Okay," Milo whispered beside her, as if he might scare the stars away. "That one is definitely a dragon."

Juniper didn't look away from the constellations. "It's not a dragon."

"It has a tail," Milo insisted, pointing. "And claws. And a face."

"That's your imagination," Juniper said.

Milo gasped like she'd insulted a royal family member. "My imagination saved Bigfoot."

Juniper turned her head toward him, and even in the dim starlight she could see his grin—wide, proud, and a little wild. Milo always looked like he was one idea away from launching himself into trouble. Sometimes that was annoying. Sometimes it was the reason they survived.

"Bigfoot saved Bigfoot," Juniper said. "We just... helped."

Milo scooted closer until their shoulders touched. “That's what C.A.T.C.H. does.”

Juniper's chest warmed at the word, even though the desert air had already started cooling. “C.A.T.C.H.” she thought. She still couldn't believe those letters were real, that her parents weren't just telling stories about it, that she'd actually *met agents* and *seen a creature with her own eyes* and helped get Bigfoot somewhere safe.

And now. Tonight. Juniper sat up slowly and looked toward the fire. It crackled quietly, orange light licking up around the edges of a blackened coffee pot. Her mom crouched near the flames and poked the coals with a stick like she was thinking hard enough to set the desert on fire with her mind.

Her dad sat on a folding chair with a small notebook balanced on his knee. He wasn't writing. He was staring at the sky too—like he was reading something written between the stars.

Blaze stood a little ways away from the group, his silhouette outlined by moonlight. His curly hair stuck out from under a cap, and his hoodie was dusted with sand from earlier when he'd insisted on “testing the ground stability for tripod placement,” which was Blaze-speak for *I tripped, but it's fine.*

He was adjusting a camera setup like a scientist preparing for a moon landing. He had a tripod, a big camera with a lens long enough to look into someone's soul, a small drone case sitting open by his feet, a stack of batteries lined up neatly like soldiers and a portable screen balanced on a cooler.

Blaze leaned closer to the camera and muttered, “If you fail me tonight, I will replace you with a toaster.”

Milo snorted. “He's talking to it again.”

Juniper couldn't stop smiling. Blaze was twelve, which meant he was just old enough to act like he was fourteen, and just young enough that you could still tell when he was excited. He tried to hide it under jokes and tech talk, but Juniper had seen the way he'd looked at Bigfoot, like it was the coolest thing he'd ever filmed and the most important thing he'd ever protected. Maybe it was

He wanted to show the world the truth. But when it came down to it, he chose to keep Bigfoot a secret to keep mythical creatures safe.

He also wanted the footage to be perfect even if it now would be seen by the agents at C.A.T.C.H.

"Blaze," Juniper called, keeping her voice low, "what are you even doing over there? The meteors aren't scheduled for another... Twenty-six minutes."

Blaze said without looking up. "Twenty-five if atmospheric conditions keep shifting like this. The wind is doing something weird."

Emmett lifted his head. "Weird how?"

Blaze tapped the side of a small device that looked like a chunky flashlight with buttons. "Like the air keeps snapping. Like static."

Juniper felt the hair on her arms rise, even though she was sitting close to the fire. Static. That word landed in her stomach like a stone in water.

Her mom glanced toward Juniper. Not worried. But alert. Megan Bell didn't do casual once she got that look.

Juniper swallowed. "It's probably just desert air," she said, though it didn't sound convincing.

Blaze finally looked up. The firelight caught his eyes, making them look bright and restless. "Desert air doesn't make my monitor flicker. Look."

He tilted the portable screen toward her. The image showed a slice of sky, magnified and crisp. Stars shone like pinpricks. And across the top edge, faint lines of interference shimmered—like invisible waves moving through space.

Milo crawled over on hands and knees. "Ooooh! That looks like TV snow."

"It's not TV snow," Blaze said. "It's like... the signal is getting..."

"...Pulled," Juniper's dad finished quietly.

Everyone got still.

Juniper turned her head. "Pulled?"

Emmett closed his notebook without snapping it, like he didn't want to make sudden noises. "When your radio cuts out right before a storm," he said, "it's because the air is charged. Electricity builds up. It can distort signals."

Milo's eyes widened. "Is there gonna be lightning?"

Her mom snorted softly. "Not out here. Not tonight."

Juniper looked between them. "Then why does it feel like...like something's waiting?" It was just a whisper because Juniper didn't want to sound like Milo when he claimed he saw dragons in the stars.

But she felt it.

The desert had been normal when they arrived—hot, bright, dusty. A place where nothing happened except sunburn and sand in your shoes. Now it felt like the whole world had leaned in closer.

Blaze stepped away from the camera and walked toward the fire, careful with his footing like he didn't want to kick sand onto his equipment.

"I know you're all being secret-agent quiet," Blaze said, "but I need somebody to tell me what's actually going on. We're camping in the middle of nowhere for a meteor shower, sure, cool, love that—"

"Love that," Milo repeated solemnly, like he was agreeing to a contract.

Blaze continued, "—but Juniper keeps staring at the ground like it's about to open up and swallow us."

Juniper's cheeks heated. "I do not."

Blaze raised an eyebrow. "You do."

Juniper crossed her arms. "I'm just...watching."

Her mom leaned back on her heels, finally looking straight at Juniper. The fire popped, sending a brief shower of sparks into the dark.

"Junebug," Megan said gently, using the nickname she always saved for serious moments and scraped knees, "tell Blaze what we told you."

Juniper's stomach fluttered. She glanced at her dad, then Milo, who looked like he was vibrating with excitement, then Blaze, who had gone very still, his teasing expression fading into something focused.

Juniper took a breath. “Grandpa buried a time capsule out here,” she said.

Blaze blinked. “Okay.”

“Not just any time capsule,” Milo blurted. “A *secret* one, we even had a secret map to find it.”

Juniper shot him a look. “Milo.”

“What? It is!” Milo insisted.

Her dad’s mouth twitched like he was trying not to smile. “It’s true,” he said. “Your grandfather was...creative.”

Blaze looked between them. “Your grandpa like—buried a box with a baseball card collection?”

Juniper shook her head. “He buried it with a date. A specific date. Tonight.”

Blaze’s eyes narrowed. “Why tonight?”

Juniper lifted her chin and tried to sound older than eleven. “Well, I think it’s because the comet passes tonight.”

Silence. Even the fire seemed to hush for a second.

Blaze stared at her. “Comet?”

Her mom nodded toward the sky. “It comes through on a predictable cycle. The meteor shower is from debris in its tail.”

Blaze's voice went quiet. "And your grandpa timed the capsule opening with a comet?"

Juniper nodded. "He said...it needed to be opened; it would be when the sky was like this."

Blaze's jaw worked like he was chewing through a hundred thoughts at once. "Okay," he said slowly. "That's...weird."

Milo lifted his hands dramatically. "It's destiny."

Juniper elbowed him.

Milo wheezed. "Owww!"

Blaze looked down at the sand, then back at Juniper. "Where is it?"

Juniper pointed—past the tents, past the ring of stones they had used to block wind from the fire to a spot marked by a circle of pale rocks arranged like a halo on the desert floor. At first glance, it looked like nothing. But Juniper had been staring at it all evening, because she could feel something under it. Not with her hands. With her bones.

The moment they arrived her mom had walked straight to that circle without checking a map. As if she already knew it too.

Blaze followed her gaze. "You're telling me there's a box under there."

Emmett stood and dusted sand off his pants. "Not a box," he said. "A capsule."

Megan rose too, smoothing her hands on her jeans. "And your grandfather didn't say what would be inside."

Juniper's heart thumped harder. "He only said it was for when... on this date when his newest descendants how had joined C.A.T.C.H. needed help."

Milo bounced on his toes. "Which is us! It has to be! We are new to C.A.T.C.H and on the right date!"

"Milo," Juniper warned.

"What? It's true." He stated.

Blaze exhaled and looked at the sky again, like he was checking if the stars were listening. "This is the part where I say it's probably nothing." Then, he grinned—sharp and excited. "But it's definitely something."

Juniper stood up, brushing sand off her legs. The air felt cooler now, but not in a normal way. It was the kind of cool that came right before something important happened. Like the desert itself was counting down.

They all walked toward the rock circle together. Juniper led. Milo followed close behind, almost stepping on her heels. Blaze carried a flashlight in one hand and his small signal scanner in the other, glancing at it like it was giving him secrets.

Megan and Emmett stayed a few steps back—close enough to protect, far enough to let the kids feel like this was theirs.

As they approached, Juniper heard it. A hum.

At first, she thought it was the wind. But the wind wasn't blowing. The night was still. The hum felt like it was coming from the ground.

Blaze slowed. "Uh," he said, voice tight. "Do you hear that?"

Milo whispered, "The desert is singing."

Juniper swallowed. "It's not singing." But she heard it too.

A low vibration in the sand, like a giant purring under the earth. Blaze raised the scanner. The screen flickered wildly—numbers spiking, then dropping, then spiking again.

"This is not normal," Blaze said, trying to keep his voice calm and failing.

Juniper stepped into the circle of rocks. The sand under her shoes felt...different. Tighter. Packed. As if it had been pressed down by something heavy. Her mom's flashlight beam swept over the ground. Nothing visible. But Juniper's skin prickled. She knelt and placed her palm on the sand. It was cool. And it buzzed faintly against her hand.

Juniper jerked back.

Milo sucked in a breath. "Juniper, did it bite you?"

"It didn't bite me," Juniper snapped, but her voice came out shaky.

Blaze crouched too, careful, like he was approaching a wild animal. "No way," he murmured.

He held his hand over the sand without touching it.
His fingers trembled slightly.

"Static," he whispered. "It's like the ground is charged."
Juniper's dad stepped closer, his expression serious now.

"Everyone back," he said.

But even as he spoke, the hum deepened.

The circle of rocks rattled. Just a little. Like someone gently tapping them from below.

Milo grabbed Juniper's arm. "Uh—Juniper?"

Juniper stared at the sand. It shifted. Not blown by wind. Not kicked by feet. Shifted like something underneath was moving.

Her mom's voice went low. "Emmett."

"I see it," her dad said.

Blaze's whisper was almost reverent. "You guys... I think it's opening."

Juniper's breath caught. A thin line appeared in the sand—straight, smooth, too perfect to be a crack. The line widened. Sand sank into it like it was being pulled down into a tiny mouth.

And then—A dull metal circle rose, slow and steady, pushing up from beneath the desert floor. No hands. No tools. Just the earth giving way like it had been waiting for a command.

The lid stopped level with the ground. For one heartbeat, everything was silent. Then a *click* sounded—clean and sharp. Like a lock releasing.

Juniper stared at the metal lid, her heart pounding so hard she felt it in her throat.

Milo whispered, "This is the coolest thing that has ever happened."

Blaze's camera light blinked from where he'd left it—like even his equipment knew it was missing the moment of a lifetime.

Juniper swallowed. The lid trembled slightly. And then, without anyone touching it, it began to unlatch. All by itself. The desert air crackled. The stars above seemed brighter. And somewhere far overhead, the first streak of a meteor ripped across the sky, white and silent, like a match struck against the universe. Juniper couldn't look away. Because whatever was inside that capsule—
It had been waiting for her. And tonight, the desert remembered.

Chapter Three – A Letter That Shouldn't Exist

No one moved. The metal lid rested half open, tilted like an eye that had just blinked awake. A thin ring of sand slid softly back into the hole around it, whispering as it settled. Juniper was the first to breathe.

"That," Milo said in a shaky whisper, "was *not* normal, but that was so cool."

Blaze stepped forward so fast he almost tripped over the ring of rocks. "Please tell me someone else saw that unlock itself."

"I saw it," Megan said quietly.

"So did I," Emmett added.

Blaze let out a breath that was half laugh, half panic. "Great. Just checking. Because if that was only me, I was about to rethink my entire personality."

Juniper knelt beside the capsule. The metal was old but smooth, the surface scratched in places like it had traveled before being buried. Faded symbols were etched around the edge—marks she didn't recognize but somehow felt familiar. Her fingers hovered above the lid.

"Juniper," her dad warned gently. "Slow."

She nodded, then looked at him. "You said Grandpa buried this for when it was time."

Her mom met her eyes. "Yes, and from what we just saw, there's no arguing that this is the right time."

Juniper swallowed. "Then this is the time."

No one argued. Juniper lifted the lid the rest of the way.
The capsule exhaled. Not air—*cold.* It rolled out in a faint mist that curled around Juniper's hands and slid across the sand. Milo squeaked and scooted back until he bumped into Blaze's legs.

"Why is it breathing?" Milo demanded.

"It's not breathing," Blaze said, crouching beside Juniper. "It's the temperature difference...probably."

"Probably is not comforting," Milo said.

Inside the capsule, everything was packed tightly, wrapped and layered with care. No random souvenirs. No jokes. No clutter. This was not just a keepsake. It was a delivery.

Juniper reached in and lifted the first item. A folded letter. The paper was thick and yellowed; the edges softened with age. Her name—*Juniper Bell*—was written across the front in dark, slanted handwriting.

"It's for you," Blaze said softly.

Milo leaned over her shoulder. "Open it. Open it. Open it."

Juniper hesitated just long enough to steady herself, then unfolded the paper. The handwriting inside was neat but energetic, like the person who wrote it never stayed still long enough to slow down.

Juniper, Milo, and Blaze,

If you're reading this, then the timing worked. That means the comet passed, the sky cracked open just enough, and you found this when you were supposed to—not too early, not too late.

Juniper's voice wobbled as she read aloud. She stopped.

Blaze frowned. "Why does he sound like he *knew* us?"

Milo tilted his head. "He didn't know us. He's our grandpa but he passed away right after mom and dad got married."

Juniper shook her head. "Shhh."

She kept reading.

You were chosen on purpose. Not because you're the oldest. Not because you're the strongest. But because you help first—and ask questions later.

Milo puffed up. "That's me."

Juniper shot him a look. "That is *not* just you."

Blaze leaned closer, eyes scanning the words. "He wrote this like instructions."

Juniper nodded and continued.

In 1947, two young travelers crashed into Earth. They were not soldiers. They were not invaders. They were teenagers.

Milo sucked in a breath. "Aliens. Didn't grandpa start C.A.T.A.C.H after he saved some aliens"

Her dad stiffened slightly but didn't interrupt.

They are being held at a place you will one day know as Area 51. The people there are afraid. And afraid people make terrible choices.

Juniper's fingers tightened on the page.

The military doesn't know what to do with them. So, they plan to take them apart to understand them.

Milo's voice came out small. "That's not okay."

"No," Juniper whispered. "It's not."

Blaze's jaw clenched. "That's not science. That's panic."

Juniper swallowed and read on.

A comet passes through this sky every forty years. It brushes against something it shouldn't—and pulls time with it when it goes. That tear is brief. Dangerous. But usable.

Blaze looked up sharply. "Time-charged wormhole."

Emmett's eyebrows rose. "That's...specific."

Blaze tapped the letter gently. "And accurate."

Juniper continued.

I sent a message once before—back in 1986. It reached the wrong moment. You felt it. But you weren't ready.

Milo frowned. "I was born in—"

Juniper stopped him with a look. Her heart was racing now.

This time is different. I am asking you to come on purpose.

Her voice dropped to a whisper. You must help them escape. You must protect them. You must help them go home.

The desert was silent except for the crackle of the fire behind them. Juniper lowered the letter slowly. "This isn't—" she started, stopped, then started again. "This isn't a coincidence."

Blaze shook his head. "No. This is a mission briefing and from what I know, maybe the very first C.A.T.C.H. mission."

Milo's eyes were huge. "We're gonna rescue aliens from Area 51."

"Yes," Juniper said firmly. "We're going to *help* them."

Her mom exhaled through her nose. "Just like Bigfoot."

Juniper nodded, then looked back into the capsule. The next item lay folded beneath the letter. A flyer jacket. She lifted it out carefully. The fabric was thick and worn, dark green with faded patches sewn onto the shoulders. Oil stains marked the cuffs. The zipper teeth gleamed dully in the firelight. On the chest, stitched in white thread, was a single word: WINGNUT

Blaze let out a low whistle. "That is an *incredible* nickname."

Juniper ran her fingers over the letters. The jacket was heavy—solid. Real.

Her dad stared at it, stunned. "That was his call sign." He tugged out his wallet and pulled out a old black and white picture of a young man in the same jacket by a plane. "This was my father when he flew planes in World War II"

Milo grinned. "Grandpa Wingnut."

Juniper slipped her arms into the sleeves. It fit. Not perfectly, it was a little long in the arms but, it looked good.

The jacket smelled faintly of metal and wind and something older—like the inside of a hangar.

Blaze's voice dropped. "Okay, that's creepy."

Juniper zipped it halfway. The weight of it settled around her shoulders, grounding her. She reached back into the capsule. Dog tags clinked softly as she lifted them free. The metal was scratched, edges dulled with time. Names and numbers were stamped deep enough to last forever.

Milo reached out and let them slide across his palm. "These were really his."

"Yes," Emmett said. "He wore them every day when I was young. Then one day they were lost, all he said was that he was sure they would turn back up. I guess they just did"

Beneath the tags lay a badge. Not military. Not police. It was a strange alloy—dark silver with a faint blue sheen that shimmered when Juniper tilted it toward the stars. The emblem etched into it wasn't familiar, but it made Juniper's chest tighten in recognition anyway.

Blaze leaned in close. "That's not from any agency I know."

Juniper flipped it over. On the back was a symbol—and a number.

Milo squinted. "What does it say?"

Juniper read aloud. "Access granted."

A final item rested at the bottom of the capsule. A narrow steel strip. Juniper lifted it. Numbers were etched into the metal, precise and sharp, like they'd been carved by a machine instead of a hand.

Blaze's breath caught. "That's a door code."

Her dad frowned. "For what door?"

Juniper didn't answer. She looked back at the letter. At the jacket. At the badge. At the code. At the sky, where meteors were now streaking faster, brighter—like the night itself was counting down.

She closed her eyes for a moment. Then she opened them. "This wasn't left behind," Juniper said steadily. "It was sent."

Blaze nodded slowly. "Across time."

Milo hugged his arms around himself, half scared, half thrilled. "So, Grandpa didn't just start C.A.T.C.H. We helped start it too."

Her mom met Juniper's gaze. "This is a lot of trust he is putting in you."

Juniper's heart pounded—not with fear, but with clarity. This wasn't an accident. This wasn't a mystery box. This was a call for help. And it had her name on it. Juniper folded the letter carefully and slipped it into the jacket pocket. Then she stood.

"Okay," she said, voice steady despite the storm of thoughts racing through her head. "So...how do we save two aliens from Area 51?"

Blaze grinned, eyes shining. "I was hoping you'd ask."

Chapter Four – No Time to Decide

The desert answered Juniper's question for them. The ground shuddered. Not a violent shake—no cracking earth or flying rocks—but a deep, rolling tremor that traveled up through Juniper's boots and into her knees, like the desert had shifted its weight.

Blaze looked straight down at the sand. "Uh. That's new."

Milo grabbed Juniper's sleeve. "Juniper?"

The air snapped. A sharp *crack*—like someone breaking a giant sheet of ice—split the quiet night. Juniper spun toward the sound just in time to see the space behind the fire ripple. Not shimmer. *Ripple.*

The darkness bent inward, folding like fabric pulled too tight. The stars behind it warped, stretching into thin lines, then snapping back into place.

Megan Bell was moving before anyone else finished inhaling. "Everyone back," she said sharply. "Now!"

Emmett stepped in front of the kids, one arm out, the other already reaching for the comm device clipped to his belt. "That's not a meteor effect."

Gristle appeared out of the shadows near the supply truck, a thermos still in his hand. His scowl deepened as he took in the sight. "Oh, I don't like that," he muttered. "I *really* don't like that.

What did I miss? I tell you I am a little late and you go and open a portal."

The ripple collapsed inward and then burst open. Light poured out. Not white. Not blue. Something in between—like moonlight mixed with lightning. The edges of the opening wavered, snapping and curling as if the air itself was struggling to hold the shape.

Milo stared, mouth open. "Is that—"

"A portal," Blaze said, voice tight but thrilled. "That is one hundred percent a portal."

Juniper's heart slammed against her ribs. The jacket felt heavier on her shoulders now, like it knew what was coming.

The portal pulsed. With each pulse, the hum grew louder, rattling the coffee pot, making the camera tripod shake. Sand lifted from the ground in tiny spirals and drifted toward the glowing opening.

Emmett spoke under his breath. "That's unstable."

"How unstable?" Megan demanded.

Blaze lifted his scanner, watching numbers spike and scramble. "Like... 'don't touch it' unstable."

The portal stretched taller, widening just enough to reveal movement inside—shadows sliding past shadows, as if the night beyond it wasn't the same night they stood in.

Juniper took one step forward.

Megan caught her arm instantly. "No."

Juniper turned. "Mom—"

"No," Megan repeated, firmer now. "Whatever that is, it's not safe."

The portal flared brighter, and a sudden *pull* yanked at Juniper's jacket, tugging the hem toward the light.

Blaze staggered, boots sliding. "Whoa—okay, that's an intake field."

Milo squeaked as his hoodie strings snapped straight out toward the opening. "Why does it want my sweatshirt?!"

Emmett grabbed Milo around the waist and hauled him back. "Everyone anchor yourselves!"

Gristle planted his boots wide and shoved a crate toward the portal to weigh it down. The crate skidded like it was on ice. "Watch out, incoming!" he barked.

Juniper looked at the opening. Then at the letter in her pocket. Then at her parents. "It's happening now," she said. "It's not waiting."

Megan's jaw tightened. "Juniper, I am not letting you walk into that thing."

The portal surged again, and this time the air screamed. Not a sound—more like pressure snapping apart. Blaze's backpack tipped over, zippers rattling wildly. He lunged for it. "Nope. Not losing this."

"What are you doing?" Emmett shouted.

Blaze swung the backpack onto his shoulders in one smooth motion. "Preparing!"

He rattled it off fast, hands moving as he spoke. "Drone case—check. Projector—check. Micro-cams—check. Power packs—check RC car —check."

Megan stared at him. "You are *not* going through that."

Blaze met her gaze. For once, he didn't joke. "I'm not letting them go alone."

Juniper's chest tightened. The pull intensified, yanking at her sleeves. She reached up and clipped the strange metal badge to the jacket without thinking. The metal warmed instantly against her chest. The dog tags followed—cool and solid as they slid over her head, settling against her collarbone.

Milo wiggled free of Emmett's grip and darted to the supply bag. "Milo!" Emmett barked.

"I'm packing!" Milo yelled back.

He shoved both hands into the open bag and stuffed his pockets until they bulged. Marshmallows. Granola bars. Something crinkly. Something chocolate.

Megan grabbed him. "Milo, stop!"

Milo looked up at her, eyes wide but steady. "We don't know how long we'll be gone."

The portal flared again. Juniper staggered forward as the pull locked onto her jacket like a hook.

Blaze grabbed her arm. "Juniper!"

"I'm okay!" she said, though her boots were sliding now.

Emmett rushed forward, grabbing Juniper's other arm. "This thing is keyed to you."

Juniper nodded, breath coming fast. "Grandpa said the timing mattered."

Megan's voice broke—just a little. "Junebug, please be careful."

Juniper looked at her mother. Really looked. At the firelight in her eyes. At the fear she tried to hide. At the trust that had always been there.

"We help first," Juniper said softly. "That's what you taught us."

The portal roared. The pull snapped hard enough that Emmett lost his footing.

Blaze yelled, "It's collapsing—whatever it is, it's *closing*!"

Gristle lunged forward grabbing Milo's backpack strap and shoving him toward Juniper and Blaze. "Go, then! Before it decides for you!"

Megan reached out, fingers brushing Juniper's sleeve. "Come back safe."

Juniper nodded, tears burning her eyes. "We will."

The ground vanished beneath them. The light swallowed everything. Milo yelped. Blaze shouted something Juniper couldn't hear. The desert tore away like a ripped photograph.

And then—

Nothing.

The portal snapped shut behind them with a thunderclap that knocked Megan and Emmett backward into the sand.

The night went quiet. Too quiet, not even a cricket chirp or a breeze. The desert looked exactly the same. Except the kids were gone.

Chapter Five – Restricted Area

Juniper hit the ground hard enough to knock the air from her lungs. Sand filled her mouth. Heat wrapped around her like a blanket straight out of an oven. She coughed and rolled onto her side, blinking against blinding sunlight.

Sunlight?

She pushed herself up on her elbows. "Why is it—"

"Hot?" Milo groaned nearby. "Why is it *so*hot?"

Blaze sat up fast, already scanning the horizon. "Okay. That was not a smooth landing. Portal time travel tech still needs work."

Juniper wiped grit from her face and looked around. The desert was the same—but wrong, it was morning. The sky was too blue. Not the deep, endless blue of home, but pale and sharp, like it had been scrubbed raw. The air smelled different too—dust and oil and metal instead of sage and smoke. And then she saw the jeeps. Three of them. Olive green. Boxy. Parked in a crooked line about fifty yards away. Sunlight flashed off their windshields, and an American flag snapped stiffly from a pole stuck in the sand. Blaze went still.

"Oh," he said quietly. "That's bad."

Milo squinted. "Why do the cars look... angry?"

"They're military," Juniper said.

As if summoned by the word, a voice barked from behind one of the jeeps.

“Hey!”

Boots crunched over gravel. A soldier stepped into view, helmet low over his eyes, rifle slung across his chest. He froze mid-step when he saw them. Three kids. One wearing an Air Force jacket. Standing in the middle of nowhere.

“What the—” he muttered, then snapped upright. “You! Don’t move!”

Another soldier appeared beside him. Then another. Juniper’s pulse roared in her ears.

Blaze raised his hands slowly. “Hi. Friendly civilians here.”

The first soldier frowned. “Civilians don’t wander onto restricted land.”

Milo leaned toward Juniper and whispered, “We’re gonna get arrested.”

Juniper hissed back, “Stop talking.”

A jeep engine rumbled to life. One soldier spoke into a radio clipped to his collar. “Yeah, we’ve got three...kids? Out by the perimeter markers.”

The word *perimeter* made Juniper’s stomach drop.

Blaze swallowed. “Okay. New plan. We smile. A lot.”

The soldiers advanced, boots kicking up dust. Juniper noticed the way they watched her jacket, their eyes snagging on the faded patches, the stitched name on her chest.

WINGNUT.

One soldier pointed. "I know that jacket. Where'd you get that coat, kid?"

Juniper opened her mouth—and had no idea what to say.

Before panic could take over, a voice cut through the tension. "Hold it."

It came from behind the soldiers. Not sharp. Not shouting. Calm. Confident. A man stepped out from between two hangar buildings that Juniper hadn't noticed before—long, low structures baked white by the sun. He wore grease-stained coveralls rolled down to his waist and a white T-shirt darkened with sweat and oil. A mechanic's rag hung from his back pocket. He walked with ease and purpose, like he belonged exactly where he was.

"Sir," one soldier said, stiffening. "This area's—"

"I know," the man said. "I fix the planes."

He stopped a few feet from Juniper. And then he saw the jacket. Really saw it. His steps slowed. His expression shifted—not fear, not anger, but recognition so sharp it looked like it hurt. He stared at the name stitched across her chest.

WINGNUT.

For a moment, the desert went quiet again.

"Where did you get that?" he whispered. So quiet that it came out just slightly louder than just mouthing the words.

Juniper's heart hammered. She looked up at him, squinting against the sun. He was young—late twenties maybe—but there was something familiar in the way he stood, the way his eyes glanced to the sky like he was always measuring distance.

"She's with me," he said suddenly. Every head snapped toward him.

The soldier nearest frowned. "Sir?"

The man didn't look away from Juniper. "They're with me," he repeated, louder now. "My niece and nephews. Family came to visit."

Blaze's mouth fell open.

Milo whispered, "We're not—"

Juniper elbowed him hard.

The soldier hesitated. "This is restricted space."

The man nodded once. "I know. I brought them out here to see the planes. My mistake."

He finally looked at the soldiers, his gaze steady. "That jacket's mine."

Juniper blinked.

The soldier looked back at Juniper, then at the man. "Sir, your name?"

"Bell," he said easily. "Nicholas Bell."

Juniper's breath caught. Nicholas. The man smiled faintly, crooked and familiar. "Most folks call me Wingnut."

Something inside Juniper clicked into place.

Milo's eyes went huge. Blaze's jaw slowly dropped.

The soldier shifted his weight, uncertain. "You should've cleared visitors."

"Yes, sir," Wingnut said. "Won't happen again."

The soldier studied him for a long moment, then sighed. "Get them out of here."

Wingnut nodded. "Already on it."

The soldiers backed away, radios crackling as they returned to their jeeps. When the engines finally faded into the distance, Wingnut turned back to the kids. He looked at Juniper's jacket again. Then at Blaze. Then at Milo. Slowly, a grin spread across his face.

"Well," he said, voice low and amazed, "this is not how I expected my day to go."

Juniper swallowed. "Hi."

Wingnut laughed—short and disbelieving. "Yeah," he said. "Hi." He glanced around, then jerked his head toward the hangars. "Let's get you out of the sun before someone asks more questions."

As they followed him, Juniper felt it deep in her bones. They weren't just in the past. They had found him. Grandpa Wingnut was real. And history had just looked straight at them—and chosen not to blink.

Chapter Six – The Man Who Fixes Planes

The hangar smelled like oil, hot metal, and sunbaked dust. Juniper noticed it the moment they stepped inside—how the heat changed, settling into something heavier, trapped beneath the curved metal roof. The space was wide and cluttered, filled with half-dismantled aircraft, tool carts, crates stamped with faded warnings, and ladders leaning wherever someone had left them last. A large screechy fan blew the air rustling posters hanging on the walls.

A propeller plane dominated the center of the hangar, its nose cone removed and its insides exposed like a patient mid-surgery. Wingnut led them in without slowing, waving the door shut behind them. The echo rang long after the metal clanged closed.

Blaze stared openly. "Wow."

Milo spun in a slow circle. "This place is amazing."

Wingnut shot them a sideways glance. "It's loud, it's hot, and it bites you if you're careless."

He reached a workbench and set his mechanic's rag down, wiping his hands slowly as if giving himself time to think. His eyes kept drifting back to Juniper's jacket.

Finally, he nodded towards it. "You want to explain how my coat walked itself into the desert?"

Juniper swallowed. "It didn't walk."

“That’s reassuring,” he said dryly.

She stepped forward. Up close, she could see the faint lines at the corners of his eyes, grease ground into his knuckles. He looked young—but tired in the way people got when they carried too many thoughts.

“It was in a time capsule,” Juniper said.

Wingnut blinked once. “A what?”

“A capsule,” Milo said quickly. “Like a buried box but way cooler. A person puts stuff in it for it to be opened on a future date.”

Blaze cleared his throat. “And we are from the future.”

Wingnut stared at him. Then he laughed. A short burst, sharp and disbelieving. “Alright. That’s a good one.”

“We’re not joking,” Juniper said.

Wingnut folded his arms. “Kid, I fix planes for the military. I don’t have time for these shenanigans.”

Blaze unzipped his backpack and pulled out his scanner. He flicked it on. The screen lit up, numbers dancing. Wingnut’s laughter died.

“What is that?” he asked quietly.

“Something that shouldn’t exist yet,” Blaze said. “At least not here.”

Juniper reached into her jacket and pulled out the letter. She held it out. Wingnut didn’t take it right away. He studied her face instead. “You look like my mother,” he said suddenly.

Juniper froze. “I...what?”

He shook his head. “Never mind.”

Then he took the letter. He read in silence. His jaw tightened. His grip on the paper went white-knuckled halfway through. When he finished, he didn’t speak right away. The hangar ticked and creaked as metal cooled.

“You’re saying,” Wingnut said slowly, “that two aliens from somewhere besides earth fell out of the sky?”

“Yes,” Juniper said.

“And they’re locked up?” he continued. “Not soldiers. Not spies.” Then he whispered to himself, “So, the rumors are true.”

“Teenagers,” Milo said. “Like... nervous ones.”

Wingnut exhaled through his nose. “I’ve heard things.”

Blaze’s head snapped up. “You have?”

“Whispers,” Wingnut said. “Late-night talk. Scientists who won’t meet your eyes. Trucks that don’t go where the paperwork says.”

Juniper leaned forward. “You didn’t believe it?”

“I believed people were scared,” he said. “That’s not the same thing.”

He stared at the plane beside them. “Fear makes folks see monsters where there aren’t any.”

A long silence stretched between them. Finally, Wingnut looked back at Juniper. “You said the letter was written by me.”

“Yes,” she nodded.

“And that I asked for help?”

“Yes.”

His mouth twisted into a half-smile. “Figures I’d rope kids into something this big.”

Blaze couldn’t help it. “You do have that energy.”

Wingnut snorted despite himself. Then his face sobered. “If they’re kids,” he said quietly, “then helping is the right thing to do.”

Juniper’s chest loosened like a knot untied.

“You’ll help us?” Milo asked.

Wingnut nodded once. “I flew planes once,” he said. “Now I listen to engines. And people.”

He grabbed his jacket from a hook off the wall—another one, newer—and shrugged into it. It had the same Wingnut name stitched on it. There was no doubt that it was the same, only it hadn’t seen as many years as the one that Juniper was wearing. “And right now,” he added, “I’m listening to you.”

The decision settled into the hangar like a promise.

Chapter Seven – Eyes in the Walls

Wingnut killed the lights. The hangar dropped into shadow, broken only by thin strips of sun slipping through high windows and the faint glow from Blaze's backpack as he knelt on the concrete floor.

"Okay," Blaze whispered, already in his element. "This is where it gets fun."

Milo crouched beside him. "This is not what Mom means when she says *have fun*."

Juniper leaned against a toolchest, arms folded inside the oversized jacket. The metal walls around them felt thicker now, closer. Like the building itself was listening.

Wingnut rested his shoulder against the hangar door, one hand on the handle. "You've got maybe eight minutes before someone wonders why I'm not fixing something loudly."

Blaze didn't look up. "Eight minutes is luxurious." He opened his pack and laid everything out with careful precision: two palm-sized drones shaped like flat insects, a tablet screen, a coil of wire, and a device that looked like it had once been a toy before he had taken it apart and rebuilt it into something smarter.

Juniper watched his hands move steadily and confidently.

Blaze didn't fidget when he worked. He focused.

"What are those?" Wingnut asked, nodding toward the drones.

“Heat-sensing scouts,” Blaze said. “They don’t just see temperature—they read patterns. Movement. Breathing. Heart rhythm.”

Milo’s eyebrows shot up. “They can see hearts?”

“Their sensors can detect heat and pulsing from a heartbeat,” Blaze said. He clipped a tiny camera module onto one drone and flipped a switch. Its surface shimmered faintly, then disappeared against the concrete.

Wingnut raised an eyebrow. “It just vanished?”

“Camouflage skin,” Blaze said. “It blends with surrounding colors.”

Wingnut let out a low whistle. “Did you build this yourself?”

“Yeah,” Blaze said. “Mostly.”

Juniper crouched beside him. “Mostly?”

Blaze shrugged. “I borrowed parts.”

Wingnut smirked. “You and I will get along just fine. I wish I had a few more mechanics like you,”

Blaze launched the first drone. It lifted silently, hovering for a second before darting toward a ventilation grate near the ceiling. Blaze’s screen lit up. Juniper leaned closer. The image shifted to grainy gray tones, then resolved into a glowing outline of metal corridors—vents running like veins through the building. Heat pulsed faintly through the walls.

Blaze tapped the screen. “Okay. Thick concrete. Reinforced steel. No windows on this side. But that’s not a problem it is still scanning well.”

Milo squinted. “That place looks like it hates fresh air.”

Wingnut nodded. “It does.”

The drone slipped deeper, passing junctions where heat flared briefly—guards walking by, engines humming, machinery cycling on and off.

Blaze dragged a finger across the map forming on the tablet. “Guard routes repeat every six minutes. Two on the upper level. Three below.”

Juniper’s pulse quickened. “You’re mapping the whole building.”

“Yup,” Blaze said. “Walls lie. Heat doesn’t.”

The second drone launched, diving into a lower vent. The screen split in two. Suddenly, one image spiked brightly. Blaze froze. Juniper felt it before he said anything—the sudden stillness, the way his shoulders locked.

“What?” she asked quietly.

Blaze zoomed in. The heat signature filled the screen. Not human. Too tall. Too narrow. Too smooth. And too hot to be human. The head shape was—elongated, with faint, branching shapes extending upward.

Milo sucked in a breath. “That’s... not a soldier.”

“No,” Blaze said slowly. “That’s not human.”

Another shape appeared beside it. Smaller. Hunched. Trembling.

Two.

Juniper's throat tightened. "That's them."

Wingnut stepped closer, his expression unreadable. "Where?"

Blaze overlaid the map. "Lower level. Behind reinforced doors. No windows. Extra cooling systems."

Wingnut's jaw clenched. "Cold rooms?"

Juniper wrapped her arms around herself. "They're keeping them chilled."

"To slow metabolism," Blaze said grimly. "And weaken them."

Milo balled his fists. "That's mean."

The drone drifted closer. The image sharpened just enough to show faint color—shimmering blues and greens rippling across the figures' skin like light on water.

Juniper felt a pang of sympathy. "They look...scared."

The smaller figure flinched suddenly, heat spiking. A human silhouette approached outside the room. Blaze pulled the drone back instantly. "Okay. We've seen enough."

The screen dimmed as he shut the video feed down. Silence filled the hangar again.

Wingnut ran a hand through his hair. "So, it's true."

Juniper met his eyes. "We told you."

He nodded once. "Yeah. You did."

Milo broke the tension. “So... step two?”

Blaze zipped his pack closed. Packing the small palm size drone away. It had silently come back. “Step two is getting closer without getting caught.”

Juniper straightened, the jacket settled around her shoulders like armor. “We found them, we just need to reach them.” she said.

Wingnut looked at the hangar door, then back at the kids. “Then we can’t waste any time.”

Outside, a plane engine roared to life. Inside the walls, two heartbeats waited.

Chapter Eight – The Cook Who Looks Away

The kitchen was the only place in the building that smelled like something meant to be alive. Steam rose from metal pots bolted to the counters. Water hissed as it struck hot surfaces. The air carried the dull comfort of bread, broth, and boiled vegetables—ordinary smells trapped inside a place that was anything but.

The cook stood alone at the center prep table. His name was Harold, though no one ever used it. Around here, he was just *the cook*. He wore a white apron stained with grease and something darker he pretended not to notice. His sleeves were rolled up, revealing arms marked by old burns and newer bruises from bumping into corners he never quite saw.

He chopped in silence. Each slice of the knife was careful, precise—like he was afraid to make too much noise.

From the hallway beyond the kitchen doors came the distant echo of boots, the sharp hiss of radios and the low hum of machines that never slept. Harold flinched every time a voice rose too loud, every time metal scraped metal.

He hated this part. Not the cooking, but who he was cooking for. He lifted a ladle and dipped it into the pot. The broth shimmered, pale and thin, giving off a faint stew smell that made his stomach turn.

"This won't be right," he muttered under his breath. He filled two trays anyway.

Harold wiped his hands on his apron and picked up the trays, one in each hand. They felt heavier than they should have. Not because of the food—but because of where he was taking them.

The corridor outside the kitchen was colder. The warmth drained away as he walked, replaced by a chill that crept into his bones. The walls here were thick, painted a dull gray that swallowed light. The overhead bulbs buzzed softly, never quite steady. He stopped in front of a reinforced door. A guard stood nearby, rifle resting against his shoulder.

"Meal delivery," Harold said quietly.

The guard nodded and unlocked the door. The cold rushed out first. Harold stepped inside. The room was small and bright, lit by lights that hummed too loudly. The floor gleamed. The air felt sharp against his skin. And in the center of the room—two figures looked up. They weren't human. Harold had seen them before, but the sight still amazed him.

Their skin shimmered in shades of blue, like polished glass dipped in moonlight. As they moved, faint hints of green and violet rippled across them, catching the light in soft waves. Neither had hair. Instead, delicate antennae curved from their heads, twitching slightly as Harold entered. One of them stood taller, posture straight despite the restraints at her wrists. Her eyes were wide and dark, reflecting the light with quiet fire. The other sat on the edge of the cot, shoulders drawn in, fingers twisting together nervously.

The taller one spoke first. "Hello again," she said.

Her voice was musical—each word carrying a soft hum, as if spoken through a vibrating string.

Harold swallowed. "Good evening."

He set the trays down slowly, careful not to meet their eyes for too long.

The smaller one leaned forward, curiosity warring with fear. "Is this food?"

"Yes," Harold said. "As best as I could make it."

The taller one tilted her head. "Thank you."

Harold nodded and turned toward the door.

"Please," the smaller one said.

He froze. He hated when they spoke to him. Not because of how they sounded—but because it made it harder to pretend they weren't people.

"Did anyone come today?" the taller one asked.

Harold hesitated. "Just the doctors."

Her antennae drooped slightly.

The smaller one's voice trembled. "They asked more questions."

Harold's jaw tightened. "I know."

The taller one studied him. "You do not like this place."

Harold let out a bitter breath. "You could say that."

She stepped closer, chains clinking softly. "We did not mean to be here."

"I know," Harold said before he could stop himself. The words hung in the cold air.

The smaller one looked up sharply. "You believe us?"

Harold closed his eyes for a moment. Then he nodded. "I heard what happened."

They leaned closer. "We were traveling," the taller one said. "I am *Zara*."

The smaller one swallowed. "I am *Kaya*"

"Our ship malfunctioned," Zara continued. "Your atmosphere interfered with our navigation. We lost control and went down."

Kayo's voice cracked. "They saw the crash. They surrounded us with lights and weapons."

Harold's hands curled into fists at his sides.

"They were shouting," Zara said. "We did not understand the language yet right away, we are fast learners."

"They tied us up," Kayo whispered. "We tried to explain."

Harold stared at the floor. "They didn't listen."

Zara's eyes softened. "You do."

Harold's throat burned. "I shouldn't but, no one listens to a cook anyway."

"But you do," she repeated.

Silence stretched between them. Finally, Harold cleared his throat. "Eat what you can. I'll...I'll come back later."

Zara nodded. "Thank you, Harold."

He flinched. "I never told you my name."

Kayo gave a small, sad smile. "You did not have to."

Harold turned away quickly, unlocking the door with shaking hands. As it sealed behind him, he leaned against the wall and closed his eyes. He told himself he couldn't help. He told himself fear was stronger than hope. But the sound of their voices followed him down the hallway, musical and innocent. And for the first time, he didn't look away.

Chapter Nine – A Car with a Voice

The corridor lights flickered once—just enough to make Harold stop walking. He frowned and turned around. The hallway behind him stretched empty and gray, the polished floor reflecting the ceiling lights in long, tired streaks. He was halfway back to the kitchen, the echo of Zara's voice still clinging to his thoughts, when he heard it. A sound that did not belong.

Whirrrr...

Soft. Mechanical. Too light to be a cart. Too steady to be footsteps. Harold leaned closer to the wall, heart thudding. The sound grew louder. Then something rolled into view. It was small. Low to the ground. Four rubber wheels. A black plastic body no bigger than a lunchbox. A toy. Harold was bewildered. He wondered how this toy was moving on its own.

Harold blinked. Then he rubbed his eyes. The little car stopped ten feet away from him. A tiny red light blinked on its front. Something like an eye.

"That's not possible," Harold whispered.

The car tilted slightly as if looking up at him. Then it spoke. "Harold? Please don't panic."

Harold yelped and jumped back so hard he smacked into the wall. "Sweet mercy—!"

“It’s okay!” the voice said quickly. A kid’s voice. A girl. Calm but urgent. “We’re not here to hurt anyone. We just need you to open a door.”

Harold stared at the car, chest heaving. “I’ve officially lost my mind.”

“You haven’t,” the voice said. “My name is Juniper.”

The car rolled forward a few inches, stopping where the overhead light was brightest.

Harold squinted. He could see it now, a camera lens mounted on top, wires tucked neatly along the sides, a radio antenna no thicker than a paperclip. He didn’t know what any of that was, but he took in everything.

“You’re...talking through a toy,” he said faintly.

“Yes,” Juniper replied. “It was the safest way.”

“Safest way for what?” Harold questioned

A second voice chimed in, quieter, a little nervous. “Also, the only way.”

“That’s Blaze,” Juniper added. “He’s driving.”

“Hi,” Blaze said. “Please don’t kick the car. We are here to help. I think you know what we are talking about.”

Harold stared at the hallway behind him, then back at the car. “This place,” he said slowly, “does things to people.”

“We know,” Juniper said. “That’s why we’re here.”

The car turned and began rolling down the corridor—toward the holding rooms. Harold hesitated. Then he followed. Each step felt heavier than the last, but he couldn't stop. The little car moved with purpose, hugging the edges of the hall, pausing whenever boots echoed nearby. When guards passed, it froze, blending into the shadows like it belonged there.

Harold's pulse hammered in his ears. If he was caught, he might be the next prisoner in this place And, he wasn't sure what he was helping with yet.

At the reinforced door, the car stopped.

Juniper's voice softened. "You have talked to them. Can you get us in closer?"

Harold nodded before realizing she couldn't see him. "I...I have to talk to them."

"That's why we chose you; we could tell that you would sympathize with them. And we could tell that you wanted to help somehow." Juniper said. "That's why we are here."

The word *chose*landed hard.

Zara's voice drifted faintly through the thick door, musical even through metal. Kayo murmured something in response.
Harold swallowed. "They don't deserve this."

"No," Juniper said. "They don't."

The car's camera angled upward slightly. "We want to get them out."

Harold let out a humorless laugh. "That's impossible."

Blaze cut in. "It's difficult. Not impossible"

“What do I need to do? I’m not saying that I will, or even that I can, but if I did, what would I need to do?” Harold rubbed his face. “After all, you’re just children.”

“Yes,” Juniper said. “So are they. All we need right now is for you to open the door”

Silence.

Harold closed his eyes. “That won’t get them out; they are locked in a cell with thick iron bars.”

“We know,” Juniper said. “We just need to talk to them first. We will make a plan later.”

“I’ve been pretending I didn’t see what was happening,” he said quietly. “Pretending it wasn’t my place.”

Juniper didn’t rush him. Blaze didn’t interrupt. Finally, Harold opened his eyes.

“What do you need?” he asked.

The car rolled closer to the door. Taking the hint, he opened the door.

Zara’s voice came clearly now, calm and steady. “You have come back.”

Harold gave a hint of a smile. “There is someone here that wants to talk to you?” he said to Zara. “I must be crazy” he said to himself.

He moved out of the way letting the remote-controlled car roll through the door and up to the bars.

"We're patched in," Blaze said his voice echoing in the larger room "Short-range audio pickup. Zara, Kayo can you take the walkie talkie off the top so we can continue talking."

"We are here to help save you" Juniper calmly said.

Kayo spoke next, his voice trembling but bright. "Our ship is nearby. You must get our ship first."

Harold leaned closer to the door. Keeping an eye on the hall. listening to the conversation between two kids that he could not see and the two alien kids behind bars.

"Where exactly is your ship?" Blaze interrupted.

"Hidden," Zara said. "Buried. They took it from us when they caught us, but the ship calls to us. It's within a kilometer of this location."

Juniper asked, "How will we find it?"

Zara paused. "When you are close to it, the air around you will feel alive."

Kayo added, "Your skin will prickle. There will be static. Like the moment before lightning."

Blaze sucked in his breath. "Electromagnetic output. Strong."

Harold nodded slowly. "I've felt that." He said as he moved from the door, over to the bars to join back in the conversation.

Juniper's voice sharpened. "Where?"

Harold hesitated, "The old storage zone. Everyone avoids it. The lights flicker and radios die in that area. It is just south of here."

"That must be it," Blaze said immediately as he adjusted his scanner to that direction. "Yes, I'm detecting something right there."

Zara's voice softened. "You will feel it before you see it."

Harold looked at the door, at the cold metal that separated him from them. "I will try and help you get closer," he said.

Juniper's voice warmed. "Thank you."

Harold shook his head. "Don't thank me yet."

He reached down and rested his hand on the cool floor beside the car. "Let's get you home," he said looking at the alien teens.

The little red light on the remote-controlled car blinked brighter. And somewhere deep in the old storage zone, the air began to hum.

Chapter Ten – The Thing That Shouldn't Fly

Wingnut's hangar had a rhythm. Metal ticking as engines cooled. Wind sneaking in through seams in the walls. Somewhere far off, a radio crackled with voices that didn't know they were wrong. Blaze loved it instantly.

"Okay, what's the plan now" Wingnut said bouncing on his heels.

"We need to make a larger drone" Blaze smiled. "This," he said, standing in the middle of the hangar with his hands on his hips, "is a *treasure chest*."

Wingnut arched an eyebrow. "It's a mess."

Blaze turned in a slow circle, eyes shining. "It's a *beautiful* mess."

Milo plopped down on an upside-down crate, swinging his legs. He peeled open a granola bar with loud determination. "Is this the part where something explodes?"

"No explosions," Juniper said automatically.

Wingnut glanced at Blaze. "No explosions?"

Blaze held up a hand. "No explosions. Just minor sparks at worst."

Juniper sighed.

Blaze was already moving—pulling open drawers, peering into bins, muttering to himself. "Okay, wing flap actuators, good! Control rods, oh wow, is this titanium?"

Wingnut crossed his arms. "That's from a P-80 Shooting Star. Bent the landing gear back in '45."

Blaze froze. "You just *had*this laying around?"

Wingnut shrugged. "You don't throw away good parts."

Blaze nodded reverently. "You're my kind of person."

Milo took another bite of his granola bar and crumbs rained down onto the concrete. "What are we building again?"

"A distraction," Blaze said. "A really large, really loud, really confusing distraction."

"How loud?" Milo asked.

"How large?" Juniper added

Blaze grinned. "Chair-sized."

Milo's eyes widened. "That's...very specific."

Juniper leaned against a workbench, watching Wingnut tighten a bolt with practiced ease. "Blaze needs something big enough to look like a UFO on radar," she explained, "but flimsy enough to crash without hurting anyone."

Wingnut snorted. "You kids plan crimes like engineers."

"We plan rescues," Juniper said quickly.

Wingnut paused.

She took a breath, then stepped closer, her voice steady but bright with feeling. "My grandfather—*your* future—started C.A.T.C.H. because he believed that fear makes people cruel. He said creatures get hunted when they're misunderstood."

Wingnut looked at her fully now.

Juniper continued, words spilling faster. "C.A.T.C.H., it stands for Creatures Agency for Tracking, Conservation, and Helping. It isn't about rules or weapons or authority. It's about choosing to help when it's easier to look away. It's about conservation. Protection. Doing the right thing even when no one's watching."

Milo raised his granola bar. "Also snacks."

Juniper smiled despite herself. "Also snacks."

Wingnut rested his wrench on the bench, jaw tight. "You talk about him like he's already...something important."

"He is," Juniper said without hesitation. "He's why we're here." Wingnut laughed softly, shaking his head. "Funny. I just fix planes."

"No," Juniper said, stepping closer. "You *listen.* You noticed rumors when others ignored them. You saw kids instead of threats. That's how it starts. Why do you think it is that I have your jacket." Then she pulled out the dog tags holding them up to him.

Wingnut hesitated but took them. Then he reached in his shirt and pulled out his dog tags. They matched. Silence settled between them, heavy but thoughtful.

Wingnut looked down at his grease-stained hands. "You're saying I don't become someone else. You are saying that I...."

Juniper shook her head. "You become *more! Y*ou must have figured this out, but Milo and I are your grandkids and you sent for us and you started C.A.T.C.H."

Milo hopped down and offered Wingnut a marshmallow. "Future you is cool."

Wingnut stared at the marshmallow like it might explain the universe.

Blaze's voice broke the moment. "Guys, I need help holding this." They turned.

Blaze had dragged two aircraft seats together, bolted to a lightweight frame, with a mess of wires, wings, and what looked suspiciously like a tail fin attached.

Wingnut blinked. "That thing will never fly."

Blaze slapped duct tape across a seam. "Correct, not for long anyways."

Juniper frowned. "Then—"

"It'll *look* like it flies," Blaze said. "Radar signature boosted, heat bloom exaggerated, sound profile tuned to scream 'unknown.'"

Milo squinted. "It looks like a chair married a plane."

Blaze nodded proudly. "That's the dream."

Wingnut circled the contraption, incredulous. "You built that... from scrap?"

Blaze wiped sweat from his forehead. "And hope." He flipped a switch. The drone hummed to life. Lights blinked. Wings adjusted. The whole thing lifted off, wobbly, loud, gloriously.

Wingnut's mouth fell open.

"Well, I'll be—" He stopped himself, then laughed, full and amazed. "That's incredible."

Blaze beamed. "Told you."

Juniper watched Wingnut's face—wonder, pride, realization all colliding at once. This was the moment. The choice.

Wingnut reached out and steadied the shaking frame. "If that thing crashes—"

"It will," Blaze said cheerfully.

"—it'll pull every jeep on base," Wingnut finished.

Juniper nodded. "That's the plan."

Wingnut straightened, shoulders squaring. He looked at Juniper. At Milo. At Blaze. At the ridiculous, impossible machine hovering in his hangar. Then he smiled. "Alright," he said. "Let's go save some aliens."

Outside, the desert wind carried the sound of engines warming. Inside the hangar, history quietly changed course.

Chapter Eleven – The Ship That Isn't a Plane

Juniper felt it before she saw anything. The air prickled. Not heat. Not cold. A crawling sensation that skimmed across her arms and crept up the back of her neck, like invisible fingers brushing past her skin. She stopped walking.

"Do you feel that?" she whispered.

Wingnut slowed beside her. His eyes narrowed, not with fear—but with focus. "Yeah," he said. "Like standing too close to a running engine."

Blaze's voice crackled softly through Juniper's earpiece. "Static levels just spiked. Like—way up."

Milo tugged at his hoodie. "It feels like my brain is buzzing." They had let themselves in by picking a lock on what looked like a small airplane hangar. From the inside it was nothing like cold clean sterile. The corridor ahead sloped downward into a forgotten section of the base. Lights flickered overhead, some burned out completely. The walls were rougher here, older, patched with mismatched panels and warning signs no one bothered to read anymore.

Wingnut lifted a hand. "This area is not on the maps they give us."

Juniper's heartbeat increased. "So...the perfect hiding place."

The hum grew louder. Blaze's drone camera feed blinked to life on Juniper's wrist screen. The image wobbled, then steadied—

revealing a wide, circular chamber carved directly into the desert rock. And in the center of it...

"Oh," Blaze breathed. "That's... beautiful."

The ship rested on the stone like it had grown there. It wasn't shaped like any aircraft Juniper had ever seen. No wings. No seams. No rivets. Its surface curved smoothly, silver-blue and softly glowing, like moonlight trapped beneath water. Faint patterns pulsed across it—slow, steady, alive.

Milo whispered, "It looks like it's breathing."

Juniper nodded. "It does."

The air around it vibrated, raising goosebumps on her arms. The hum wasn't loud, it was *present*, filling the space in a way sound usually didn't.

Wingnut stepped forward, awe flickering across his face. "That's not metal," he murmured. "Not like ours."

Blaze cut in, urgent. "Okay, problem. Guards are moving this way."

Juniper stiffened. "How many?"

"Too many," Blaze said. "Which means it's distraction time."

"Distraction," Milo said eagerly. "I can do distraction!"

Blaze laughed under his breath. "Buddy, you already are one."

A whirring sound echoed as Blaze launched a drone from the vent above. It zipped out into the open, lights blazing, letting off a sharp electronic pulse that crackled through the chamber. Every radio nearby shrieked.

“What’s going on?” a distant voice shouted.

The drone continued upward through an access shaft, streaking toward the surface.

Blaze grinned. “Meet my Unidentified Aerial Phenomenon, gentlemen. Or given the date I should say Unidentified Flying Object. Once this small one makes it to the larger drone, it will connect at the top and take everyone on a wild goose hunt.”

Boots thundered overhead. Radios barked orders. Engines roared to life. Milo pumped his fist. “They took the bait!”

Wingnut didn’t waste a second. “You two—inside. Now.”

Juniper ran toward the ship. As she approached, the glow brightened, responding to her presence. A section of the hull shifted seamlessly, unfolding into an opening without hinges or doors.

Her breath caught. “It knows we’re here.”

Wingnut’s eyes shone. “Good. It’s listening.”

They stepped inside. The interior was nothing like a cockpit. No chairs. No dials. No switches. The space curved around them, walls glowing softly, the floor warm beneath their boots. Symbols drifted through the air like holograms made of light and motion rather than glass.

Juniper spun slowly. “Okay. None of this makes sense.”

Wingnut laughed—a short, amazed sound. “That’s flying for you.”

Blaze’s voice crackled. “Please tell me there’s a steering wheel.”

Juniper stared at the floating shapes. They shifted as she moved, responding to her gaze. “It’s not a steering wheel,” she said slowly. “It’s...intention based.”

Wingnut tilted his head. “Say that again.”

Juniper stepped forward. The lights brightened where her hand hovered. “In video games, the best controls don’t fight you. They respond. You don’t *push* the ship—you *think* where you want to go and the ship responds.”

Wingnut’s grin spread. “You fly with instinct.”

“Yes,” Juniper said. “And muscle memory.”

Wingnut stepped beside her. “I fly with balance. Pressure. Trust.”

He placed his hand against the glowing wall. The ship responded. The hum deepened. The floor shifted gently, like a breath drawn in. Outside, alarms wailed.

Milo’s voice crackled through the comm. “Guys? They’re coming back!”

Juniper closed her eyes. Up, she thought. Away. The symbols flared. The ship lifted—not with a jolt, not with a roar—but with a smooth, effortless rise, as if gravity had simply let go.

Wingnut laughed again, louder this time. “She flies like a dream.”

Juniper opened her eyes as they crashed through the ceiling. The chamber fell away beneath them. They were airborne. And the impossible ship had chosen them to fly it.

Chapter Twelve – The Kitchen Lie

The sky tore itself open. From the cockpit, Juniper saw the first streak of fire slash across the darkness—white-hot, silent, impossibly fast. Another followed. Then three at once.

"The meteor storm's starting," Blaze said over the comm, his voice tight with awe. "Timing's perfect. Also, terrible."

Wingnut guided the ship downward, hands steady, eyes locked on the base below. "Hold on."

The ship didn't shake. It *listened.* Juniper felt the hull respond as if it understood urgency. The glow dimmed, the hum softened, and the world tilted gently as they descended. The roof rushed up to meet them. The ship touched down without a sound.
No clang. No scrape. Just a quiet *settling,* like a bird folding its wings.

Milo's voice crackled through the channel. "That was smoother than Dad parking the car."

Wingnut grinned. "She's got good manners."

Outside, alarms wailed—confused, overlapping. Soldiers shouted. Radios crackled with half-finished orders. Juniper unzipped the jacket and pulled out the badge. It felt warm in her palm now, almost alive.

"Ready?" she asked.

Wingnut nodded. "Go."

She ran to the roof access door. The metal was thick, reinforced, and painted dull gray. A keypad glowed faintly beside it. Juniper pressed the badge flat against the panel. The light flickered. She slid the steel strip from her pocket and typed the code, fingers moving fast.

Beep. The door unlocked.

Juniper exhaled. “We’re in.”

They slipped inside just as another meteor flared overhead, lighting the corridor through narrow windows like a camera flash.

The hallway below was chaos. Red lights pulsed. Boots thundered. Voices echoed from every direction. Blaze’s hologram projector whirred to life behind them.

“Launching distraction in three,” Blaze said. “Two–,” a life-sized image flickered into existence at the far end of the hall: a glowing, unmistakably alien silhouette sprinting past the intersection. “–one.”

“CONTACT!” Someone shouted.

Guards surged chasing after the illusion, boots pounding as radios erupted.

Juniper’s heart raced. “It worked.”

Wingnut nodded sharply. “Move!”

They sprinted down the opposite corridor, footsteps swallowed by alarms. At the holding room, Juniper slid to a stop. Two guards stood watch.

Blaze whispered, “Give me ten seconds.”

Juniper rolled a small hologram puck across the floor. It burst into light, sparks, smoke and the image of a malfunctioning panel screaming warnings.

"What in the world?" One guard said, turning.

Wingnut moved like he'd practiced this a thousand times. He bumped into the other guard just hard enough to distract him, murmured an apology and Juniper's hand darted out, snatching the key ring from the man's belt.

The alarm screamed louder.

"Hey!" the guard shouted.

Juniper didn't look back. The door flew open. Zara and Kayo stood frozen inside, eyes wide.

Juniper rushed forward. "It's us. We're getting you out."

Zara's antennae lifted sharply. "You came."

Kayo's voice shook. "We felt the ship."

Juniper quickly began the work of unlocking everything. First the cell doors and then the shackles binding the prisoners.

Behind them, footsteps thundered closer. Then a voice echoed down the hall—loud, desperate, shaking with purpose.

"They're in the kitchen!" Every guard froze.

"What?"

"The *kitchen!*" the voice shouted again. "I saw them—run!" Boots turned. Shouts redirected. The sound of pursuit veered away. Juniper spun.

The voice was Harold, the cook. He stood in the doorway, chest heaving, eyes bright with fear and courage tangled together. "Go," he said. "Now."

Zara stepped forward and wrapped her arms around him. "Thank you," she said, her voice a soft chord of sound.

Kayo joined them, trembling.

The cook swallowed hard and hugged them back, quickly and fiercely. "Get home safely."

He pulled back and thrust something into Milo's hands. A ladle. Old. Heavy. Dented. Milo blinked. "Uh—thanks?"

The cook smiled sadly. "So, you remember me."

Juniper stared at him—really looked. The shape of his jaw. The slope of his shoulders. The stubborn kindness etched into his face. He almost looked like a young Gristle. The recognition startled her briefly.

Blaze shouted from the hall, "Time!"

They ran. Behind them, the cook turned and walked calmly toward the kitchen, shouting again to draw attention away. Juniper didn't look back. The ship was waiting. And the sky was still falling.

Chapter Thirteen – The Sky Opens

The night exploded into motion. Juniper burst out onto the roof first, lungs burning, boots skidding across concrete still warm from the day. Wingnut, Blaze, Milo, Zara and Kayo were close behind. Wind whipped around them, tugging at Juniper's jacket, carrying the sharp smell of ozone and dust. Above them, the sky was on fire.

Meteors streaked across the darkness in blazing arcs, white and gold, tearing open the heavens like sparks from a grinding wheel. The desert glowed faintly below, lights blinking in frantic patterns as alarms wailed across the base. Wingnut waited at the ship; one hand pressed to the hull.

"Everyone together!" Wingnut shouted. "Get on the ship quickly!"

Kayo and Zara were first to enter the ship. Blaze, Juniper and Milo stopped in their tracks hesitating as they looked back at Wingnut who had stopped behind them.

"Are you coming with us?" she asked.

Wingnut smiled, "I belong in this time Juniper. But don't worry, we will meet again and I will be more prepared next time!"

Milo darted back towards Wingnut and threw his arms around him. "I can't wait to spend more time with you grandpa Wingnut!"

Wingnut's eyes watered slightly as he returned the hug and pulled Juniper and Blaze in to join the embrace.

"This whole C.A.T.C.H. thing you mentioned has been weighing on my mind. I've always wanted to find a way to help those who need it. Especially those who are misunderstood, feared, trapped or hunted."

Juniper's eyes watered as well, "That's what C.A.T.C.H. is all about and you are its founder."

"But how does it all happen?" Wingnut asked.

A deep hum answered him. The ship's glow intensified, patterns racing across its surface like light flowing through veins as it lifted off and hovered above them.

Wingnut shifted his focus to Blaze and his future grandchildren, "Your way home is leaving." He pushed them away as he backed away from them. "Return safely! I'll be thinking of you every day until you are officially born in this timeline."

Juniper felt the pull instantly, gently but firm, like a current in water.

"Whoa," Milo said as his feet lifted off the ground. "I'm floating!"

The tractor beam had caught them all at once. Juniper's stomach flipped as gravity let go. She clutched Milo's arm as they rose, the world tilting beneath them.

Blaze laughed—half thrilled, half in disbelief—as his backpack swung forward as he smiled and waved. "This beats the elevator," he said breathlessly.

Wingnut waved back at them as they were pulled into the hovering ship.

Zara's antennae shimmered as she looked up from the ships controls as Milo, Juniper and Blaze set their feet on the solid surface of the ship's bridge. They noticed a small glowing shape that had joined Kayo and Zara bounding around their legs watching the visitors as they were pulled inside the ship.

Milo was puzzled as he gasped. "Is that a dog? Where did it come from?" Noticing the two small antennae on the dog's head he continued. "It's an alien dog!"

Zara laughed, "He has been taking care of our ship while we were prisoners."

The very unique dog's body pulsed with soft light, tail wagging wildly as it approached Milo, hovered up to his face and licked it in midair.

"Hey—hey!" Milo sputtered, laughing. "Personal space!"

The ship began to ascend faster. Boots thundered below onto the roof, guards shouting as rifles lifted uselessly toward the sky.

"Stop!" Wingnut yelled. "Hold your fire!"

The ship surged faster towards the night sky.

Juniper grabbed a curved support as the interior lights flared. The walls shifted color, responding to hands on the controls—Zara and Kayo moving forward with skilled confidence.

"Orbit protocols," Zara said, her voice clear and resonant.

Kayo's fingers danced through the glowing symbols, his earlier fear replaced by focus. "Aligning with standard orbit vector."

Blaze stared, awestruck. "They're flying it like it's alive."

“It is alive,” Juniper realized.

The hum deepened into something powerful. The ship shot upward. Through the transparent arc above them, Juniper watched Earth fall away—runways shrinking, buildings flattening, the desert stretching out like a painted map.

Milo pressed his face to the view. “We’re leaving the planet.”

“It’s so beautiful!” Juniper reacted.

The sky darkened from indigo to velvet black. Stars burst into clarity. Juniper felt her breath catch—not with fear, but with wonder.

With the earth far below, they had escaped.

The only thing left to do, figure out how to make it back to her parents who were in the future.

Chapter Fourteen – The Ladle

Space was quiet in a way Juniper had never known. Not empty—*vast*. The stars didn't flicker here. They burned steadily and sharp, scattered across the black darkness like lanterns hung by careful hands.

The ship glided forward without effort, its glow softening now that the danger had passed. Milo sat cross-legged on the warm floor, still holding the ladle. The glowing dog circled him, first while levitating in the air and then down to the surface as feet lightly made contact as it plopped down and next to Milo. It wagged its tail so hard its whole body wiggled.

"Okay," Milo said solemnly, "you are officially my favorite space creature."

The dog answered by licking his face.

"Hey—hey!" Milo laughed, wiping his cheek. "Why are you so sticky?"

The dog glowed brighter. Not blinding—just warmer, like a nightlight turned up a notch.

Blaze blinked. "Did it just...react?"

Zara knelt nearby, antennae swaying gently. "It responds to kindness. And he clearly likes Milo a lot!"

Milo beamed and dug into his pocket. "Good news. I come prepared." He pulled out a slightly squished marshmallow and held it out. The dog sniffed, tail wagging faster, then gently took it. The glow intensified.

Juniper stared. “It’s feeding off joy.”

Kayo nodded. “And generosity.”

Milo puffed out his chest. “I’m very generous.”

Wingnut laughed softly, leaning against the curved wall. “That’s affirmative.”

Juniper’s gaze drifted to the ladle in Milo’s lap. It was scratched and dented, the handle worn smooth by decades of use. She reached out and wrapped her fingers around it. The moment she touched it, something clicked.

“This feels...familiar,” she murmured.

Blaze glanced over. “How familiar?”

“Like,” Juniper said slowly, “I’ve seen it before.”

Wingnut straightened. “Let me see that.”

He turned the ladle over, studying the handle. There, barely visible beneath layers of wear, was a small mark—a few letters carved by a careful hand.

“H.G.R.” Wingnut said.

Juniper’s breath caught. “Gristle has one like it. He has a set and I think this is the missing one.”

Blaze’s eyes widened. “The cook.”

Milo froze. “Wait. You mean the guy who helped us?”

Juniper nodded, heart pounding. “He looks like him. The same build. The same eyes.”

Wingnut exhaled, something like awe softening his voice. “Then that was his grandfather too.”

“More like his father or uncle” Blaze stated.

Milo looked down at the ladle like it had just become magic. “So, he was part of C.A.T.C.H. too.”

Juniper shook her head gently. “Maybe not officially.”

Zara stepped closer, her voice warm. “But he chose to help.”

Kayo smiled faintly. “That is how legacies begin.”

The ship hummed softly around them, carrying them farther from Earth. Juniper held the ladle tighter. Some things weren’t passed down in words or titles. Some things were carried forward in simple choices. And now, the proof rested in her hands.

Chapter Fifteen – A Gift to Remember

The ship slowed. Not abruptly—nothing about it ever was—but with a gentle easing, like a breath being carefully let out. The glow along the walls dimmed from bright blue to a softer hue, and the steady hum beneath Juniper's feet shifted into a lower, almost mournful tone.

Zara straightened. Kayo lifted his head sharply, antennae flicking.

"It is time," Zara said.

Juniper felt her chest tighten. "Already?"

Kayo nodded. "The comet's path is changing. The window it opened is closing behind us."

Blaze glanced at his screen, fingers flying. "Yeah. I'm reading a massive drop in temporal energy. Like someone slowly zipping reality shut."

Milo hugged the glowing dog closer. "Does that mean we're... stuck here?"

"No," Zara said gently. "It means we must say goodbye."

The words settled into the ship like falling snow—quiet, heavy, unavoidable. Wingnut stepped back, giving the kids space. He removed his cap and held it against his chest; eyes fixed on the stars beyond the hull. "Don't worry kids I will find a way to reach out to you. After all, I did it once. I can do it again. I have time to figure it out."

Zara turned to Juniper. "You did not hesitate."

Juniper shook her head. "Neither did you."

Kayo stepped forward, voice trembling but strong. "On our world, bravery is measured by how much you protect others—not how much you conquer."

Blaze swallowed. "Then you'd fit right in with C.A.T.C.H."

Zara smiled, her skin shimmering brighter for a moment. "We will remember you. Always."

Milo sniffed. "You better."

The dog wiggled out of Milo's arms and trotted toward Zara, tail glowing softly. It circled her once, then Kayo, letting out a low, musical sound.

Zara knelt, placing both hands on its head. "Ah, Little Light," she whispered, her voice thick. "Do you want to stay on earth?"

Milo's eyes widened. "Stay...stay?"

Kayo nodded. "It bonded with you and we'd like to leave a gift for the courage and kindness you have all showed us."

The dog bounded back to Milo and pressed against his legs, glowing brighter than ever.

Juniper's throat burned. "Are you sure?"

Zara rose slowly. "It will be safe with you. Loved. And it will remind you that you were not alone."

Milo hugged the dog fiercely. “I promise I’ll take care of you. I’ll share snacks. And blankets.”

The dog licked his face in agreement.

Blaze wiped his eyes quickly. “Okay, wow. Did not expect space to make me emotional.”

Kayo spoke up, “This is a very special dog. On our world the name of his species translates in your language to ‘mimic.’ He is able to take other forms. So be aware of that”

Blaze reacted, “A shapeshifter?”

“Within limits.” Kayo said, “His DNA is programmed to be able to take on any form within his species. On earth, all of the forms he can shift into would be classified as *canus lupus familiaris*. Basically, he can appear like any kind of dog he wants to mimic.”

Milo smiled, “He is officially the best dog ever!”

Blaze looked puzzled, “What about you two Kayo and Zara? Are you able to shapeshift too?”

Kayo smiled, “Within similar limits, yes.”

Blaze’s eyes were wide with wonder, “I would love to learn more about how that works.”

Zara stepped closer to Juniper and placed a glowing hand over her heart. “One day we will return to your planet, and we can learn more about each other. Your kindness has crossed time and space.”

Juniper nodded, tears slipping free. “Yours has too.”

The ship hummed again—more urgently now. Kayo backed toward the glowing symbols forming a new doorway of light. "We must go."

Milo took a step forward. "Wait—"

Zara smiled sadly. "Goodbyes are not endings. This new circle of friendship that we have created will endure in our minds and hearts forever."

Then the light flared. Zara and Kayo watched as the three kids and an alien space dog stepped into it together, their forms dissolving into shimmer and sound, like music fading into silence.

The ship shuddered gently. The hum softened. Juniper stared at the place where they'd stood, heart aching—but warm. They hadn't lost them. They had helped them home. And sometimes, that was the greatest gift of all.

Chapter Sixteen – What We Carry Home

The desert night returned in a rush of wind and light. Juniper stumbled forward as the portal released them, boots sinking into familiar sand. The cool air wrapped around her like a memory, carrying the smell of sage and smoke. The fire still burned low in its ring of stones, glowing red instead of wild and bright. They were home.

Milo laughed first, one short, disbelieving sound. “We didn’t die.”

Blaze staggered to his knee, bracing himself with one hand. “Give it a minute. My legs are still in space.”

The glowing dog bounded out of the fading light and shook itself, sending sparks of soft blue across the sand before curling up at Milo’s feet.

“Still glowing,” Milo announced proudly. “Good dog.”

The portal collapsed with a quiet snap, like a book closing. For a moment, the desert was silent. Then Megan Bell ran towards the returned group. She crossed the sand in three strides and pulled Juniper into her arms so tightly that Juniper could barely breathe.

Milo disappeared into the hug too, squished between them was the space dog. Everyone laughed and protested at the same time.

“You don’t get to do that to us ever again,” Megan said fiercely, her voice shaking.

Emmett joined them, one hand on Juniper's shoulder, the other resting on Milo's head. He didn't say anything at first. He just breathed, like he was counting heartbeats.

"Mom, Dad, meet Sparky our new pet. Technically, we must keep him since he is an alien creature that we are protecting." Milo said as Sparky licked his face.

Megan and Emmett looked at each other.

"Well, since the cute antennae on Sparky prove he's an alien, we will consider letting you keep him," Megan said. "And we will talk more about this later young man. An alien dog on earth will need more protecting that you realize."

Emmett said, "What do alien dogs eat?"

Milo announced, "Well I know he eats marshmallows."

Juniper laughed, "I'm sure Gristle can help you with a nutritious space dog diet."

Gristle was standing back a few steps from the group, "Just keep that dog out of the kitchen."

Blaze, recovering from the time travel re-entry, pushed himself upright and gave an awkward wave. "Uh, Hello? Successful unauthorized time mission accomplished."

Emmett huffed out a laugh despite himself.

Gristle's eyes with his usual scowl caught a glimpse of something in Milo's hands. It was the ladle.

"That," Gristle said slowly, "looks familiar."

Milo held it up. "It's from the cook at military base in 1947."

Gristle's scowl faltered. Juniper stepped forward. "He helped us. He...looked like you."

Gristle reached out, hesitated, then took the ladle. His fingers traced the worn handle. He looked closely at the small carved letters near the end of it, "H.G.R." he whispered.

The desert wind stirred. Gristle swallowed. "My father used to cook for half the town. Said food was how you kept people human." He cleared his throat. "I always knew he stood for something."

Silence settled—not heavy, but full.

Megan glanced at Emmett, then back at the kids. "You made the right choice."

Juniper nodded. "That's what C.A.T.C.H. does."

Emmett smiled softly. "Then C.A.T.C.H. didn't start in a lab?"

Juniper looked at the stars overhead, at the comet's fading trail. "It started with a choice," she said.

The glowing dog nudged Milo's leg. Milo grinned. "And snacks."

They laughed together, the sound drifting out into the desert—proof that some things, once carried forward, never fade.

Epilogue – Official Business

The next day was filled with a full mission report from Juniper, Blaze and Milo. Megan, Emmett and Gristle listened intently as their two agent children and candidate agent Blaze described their experiences in great detail and responded to many questions.

That night as they sat around the campfire, the desert was quiet again. Not the tense, waiting quiet of portals and falling stars—but the kind that settled in after something important had ended.

The fire had burned down to glowing embers, and the sky above Nevada stretched wide and ordinary, as if nothing impossible had happened there at all.

Sparky floated lazily a few inches off the ground, glowing a soft blue as he chased his own tail. Every so often he drifted too high, panicked for half a second, and then plopped back down in the sand with a pleased little chirp.

Milo clapped. "See? Perfectly normal dog."

Juniper raised an eyebrow. "Normal dogs don't hover."

Sparky wagged his tail harder in protest.

Blaze sat cross-legged near the fire, a tablet balanced on his knees. He was half-listening, half-typing, already running diagnostics on three devices that technically should not have survived time travel.

Every few seconds, Sparky wandered over and nudged his elbow with a glowing nose.

"Yes, yes, you're very helpful," Blaze muttered. "Please stop recharging my batteries without asking."

Sparky chirped proudly and glowed brighter.

Emmett Bell had stepped away from the group briefly and then returned. He cleared his throat loudly looking directly at Blaze.

Blaze looked up immediately.

When Emmett cleared his throat like that and used that tone, it usually meant one of two things: *mission briefing* or *you're in trouble*.

Blaze braced himself for either.

Emmett stood a few steps away, holding a thin black folder stamped with the familiar silver emblem and the words:

C.A.T.C.H.
Creatures Agency for Tracking, Conservation, and Help
Official Business

Gristle leaned against a tree just outside the circle nearby, arms crossed, pretending not to watch. Megan stood up with Juniper and Milo, smiling in that quiet way that meant she already knew this moment mattered.

"Sparky," Emmett said calmly, "why don't you go over and play with Milo for a minute?"

The space dog tilted his head, considered this, then bounced over and promptly got tangled in Milo's hoodie strings.

"Good enough," Emmett said.

He turned back to Blaze.

"Blaze," he continued, "you were invited on this mission as an applicant."

Blaze nodded. "Yes, sir. Junior agent candidate. Provisional. No cape."

"And yet," Emmett said, opening the folder, "during an unauthorized time displacement, you designed and deployed reconnaissance drones, bypassed mid-century military surveillance, mapped a classified facility using heat signatures alone, built a functional distraction craft out of scrap aircraft parts, and remotely coordinated a multi-species extraction."

Blaze swallowed. "When you say it like that, it sounds...reckless."

Gristle snorted. "It was."

Emmett smiled slightly. "It was also brilliant."

Blaze froze.

Emmett reached into the folder and removed a single, heavy certificate—thick paper, embossed with the C.A.T.C.H. seal. A second attachment was clipped beneath it: a narrow strip of metal etched with fine symbols and circuitry.

"Blaze," Emmett said, "C.A.T.C.H. was founded on one rule: help first. You didn't just follow that rule. You expanded what it means."

He handed the certificate to Blaze. It read:

C.A.T.C.H. AGENT CERTIFICATION
This document recognizes Blaze Zuko as an Official Junior Agent of C.A.T.C.H. with full field status.

Blaze stared. "Wait—official?"

"With conditions," Emmett added dryly. "You're still twelve."

"That's fair," Blaze said quickly.

Emmett clipped the metal strip to the bottom of the certificate. "This," he continued, "is a Special Agent Technical Endorsement. It recognizes advanced aptitude in non-standard engineering, adaptive problem solving, and...frankly, building things no one else would think to build."

Gristle leaned forward. "It also means if something breaks, you're fixing it."

Blaze grinned. "Deal."

Emmett met Blaze's eyes. "You don't just build tools, Blaze. You build *options*. You gave people—and creatures—a way out."

Blaze's voice went quiet. "I just didn't want them to be scared."

Emmett nodded. "Exactly."

From behind them, Sparky bounded back over to Blaze, glowing brighter as if he sensed the moment. He sat—mostly—then gently placed one glowing paw on Blaze's knee.

Zara's voice echoed faintly in Blaze's memory: *He responds to kindness.*

Emmett glanced down at the alien dog. "As for our newest... associate..."

Sparky wagged so hard he lifted off the ground.

“Zara and Kayo made their choice,” Emmett said. “Sparky stays on Earth—as a protected extraterrestrial lifeform under C.A.T.C.H. jurisdiction.”

Milo gasped. “So he’s—”

“A C.A.T.C.H. asset,” Emmett finished.

Sparky chirped proudly.

“And,” Emmett added, “given his unique energy signatures, he’ll have the option of entering training as a field companion.”

Sparky immediately sat beside Blaze as if standing at attention.

Blaze blinked. “Oh no.”

“Oh yes,” Juniper said, grinning.

Emmett smiled. “Looks like you’ve been chosen.”

Sparky licked Blaze’s face, glowing happily.

Blaze laughed, wiping his cheek. “Okay. But just so we’re clear—I do *not* do chew toys.”

The dog chirped and floated a marshmallow into Blaze’s hand.

Gristle huffed. “I’m still not letting that thing in my kitchen.”

Sparky’s glow dimmed slightly.

“...At least while I’m cooking,” Gristle amended.

Emmett smiled, “So Blaze, with your technical endorsement you will have the opportunity to support many missions in various capacities - from C.A.T.C.H. headquarters, from one of the C.A.T.C.H. regional science stations and directly as you have done as a junior field agent. Congratulations!”

The group applauded as Emmett shook Blaze’s hand.

Blaze smiled from ear to ear. “Thank you Agent Bell, and thanks to all of you for supporting and believing in me!”

“What’s our next mission?” Milo asked.

Emmett smiled looking at Megan and then at Gristle. “What I can say right now is all of us except Blaze and Sparky will be going back to Utah. Well Utah and Idaho. Bear Lake along the border is the location of our next assignment. Blaze and Sparky will be going to our C.A.T.C.H. Rocky Mountain Support Base where Sparky will begin his training and Blaze will support us remotely using some of our new technology.”

Juniper and Milo looked at each other.

“No way!” Milo said.

“Is it the Bear Lake Monster dad? Juniper asked.

“I’ll brief you all tomorrow as after we break camp and are on our way,” Emmett said.

As the fire began to die, the desert wind stirred, carrying the last trace of starlight across the sand. Above them, the sky was quiet. But the work of C.A.T.C.H.—and the bonds it created—had only just begun.

Other Books by Eugene Fuller

When strange sightings and unexplained creatures start making headlines, the young agents of C.A.T.C.H. are called in for their first official mission—Operation Bigfoot. Armed with gadgets, grit, and a healthy dose of courage, they head into the wilderness to uncover the truth behind the legend. *Case #1: Operation Bigfoot* is a fast-paced adventure packed with mystery, teamwork, and just enough campfire chills to keep readers turning pages late into the night.

In a forgotten corner of the countryside, a small schoolhouse holds secrets that refuse to stay buried. When a group of children emerge from the mist, two reluctant guardians are forced to confront a chilling mystery that blurs the line between memory and madness. *Children of Desperation* is a haunting tale of loss, redemption, and the terrifying cost of being forgotten.

www.ingramcontent.com/pod-product-compliance
Lightning Source LLC
LaVergne TN
LVHW090616110826
845146LV00001B/412

* 9 7 9 8 9 9 4 3 9 9 6 4 4 *